Coconut
Comes to School

For the Lacy boys, Ted, Alan and Roy,
and all their families, B.D.

To Molly and James, I.B.

First published in Great Britain by HarperCollins Publishers Ltd in 2002

1 3 5 7 9 10 8 6 4 2

ISBN: 978-0-00-782688-9

Text copyright © Berlie Doherty 2002
Illustrations copyright © Ivan Bates 2002

The author and illustrator assert the moral right to be identified
as the author and illustrator of the work.
A CIP catalogue record for this title is available from the British Library.

The HarperCollins website address is: www.harpercollins.co.uk

Printed and bound in China

Coconut
Comes to School

Written by Berlie Doherty ✑ *Illustrated by Ivan Bates*

HarperCollins*Publishers*

Coconut comes to school every day.

She lives at the other side of the
woods, in a field full of bobbing rabbits
and badger tracks. And she comes to
school with Mrs Pie.

Hee-haw! Coconut's hooves

snap twigs in the bluebell woods.

The squirrels peer from trees.

In the school across the fields

the children are listening.

Hee-haw! Coconut trots through the dewy-wet grass.

Mice shiver their whiskers.

In the classroom the children whisper, "She's coming! Coconut's coming!"

Hee-haw! Coconut scrambles across the ditch.

The children smile at each other.

"She's coming! Coconut's coming!"

Hee-haw!

Coconut canters across the school meadow.

Her hooves go *trit* trot *trit* trot.

Her ears go *flip* flap *flip* flap.

Her tail goes *swish* as she flicks at the flies.

swish *swoosh*
swish *swoosh*

"She's here! Coconut's here!"

the children laugh.

Mrs Pie runs behind Coconut. Her face is full of smiles. She goes to the kitchen and gets down her pots and pans.

Coconut puts her long nose through the classroom window.

Hee-haw! Hee-haw!

Her eyes are brown like chestnuts. Her hair is dark like the bark of trees, and rough as a brush to touch. Her lips go *slip-slop-slap*.

"Hello Coconut!" the children call.

But Mr Clapper the teacher shouts, "Go away Coconut! Go back home! Donkeys can't come to school!"

Coconut backs away and lowers her head.

Flip-flop, her long ears flap.

Swish-swoosh, her long tail swings.

Mr Clapper tries to shoo her away. "Go on! Go back home!" he shouts. But Coconut munches the grass and swings her head this way and that way.

"Donkeys can't come to school," Mr Clapper

tells Mrs Pie. "Don't bring her again."

Mrs Pie smiles in the steamy kitchen

that smells of apples and jam.

"The children love Coconut," she says.

"And Coconut loves them."

"Well, I don't love her,"

Mr Clapper says. "I don't love

her one bit. Coconut must go!"

The next day, he thinks of a plan to make Coconut go away. He comes to school with a bag of carrots tucked under one arm and a rope in his pocket. He hides them in his desk.

While the children are eating their dinner, Mr Clapper creeps over to where Coconut is munching the grass.

"Here you are, Coconut," says Mr Clapper. "Juicy carrot!"

Coconut sniffs at the carrot and chomps her teeth.

Mr Clapper steps back and dangles the carrot in the air.

Coconut steps forward.

Sniff! goes her nose.

Chomp! go

her teeth.

"Follow me, Coconut. Follow me," says Mr Clapper. "You can have all the carrots you want. I'll tie you to a tree in the bluebell woods and you can wait for Mrs Pie to come home. What a happy donkey you'll be, watching the squirrels play, and eating those carrots all day long."

He holds up the carrot again. Coconut steps forward.

Sniff! Chomp!

Mr Clapper steps back. "Juicy carrot, juicy carrot," he says.

Sniff! Chomp!

And so they go on, over the meadow of buttercups and daisies. Mr Clapper walks backwards, "Juicy carrot! Juicy carrot." Coconut ambles after him.

Sniff! Chomp!

But oh! The ditch! Mr Clapper
tumbles down into it, toes
over nose. The carrots
fly this way and that like
a shower of golden
fish. And there he lies
with his eyes
closed tight.

"Help!" he shouts. "Oh! My poor foot! Oh, how it hurts! Help! Help!"

But no-one can hear him, so far from the school. No-one can see him, tucked in the ditch like a bundle of washing. "Nobody knows where I am. No-one will rescue me! I'll be here for ever!" he moans.

And then he hears the best
sound in the world.

trit *trot*

trit *trot*

chomp!

sniff!

chomp!

swi

Something warm and wet nuzzles Mr Clapper's ear.

Something as tickly as feathers strokes his chin.

"Coconut! You're going to save me!
Nice Coconut! Kind Coconut!"

Coconut lowers her head, and
Mr Clapper heaves himself on to
her back. And they trot
slowly over the meadow.

Mrs Pie wraps Mr Clapper's poor foot in bandages and gives him a cup of hot, sweet tea.

"How clever of Coconut to find you!" she says. "How did she know you were there?"

But Coconut just nods and nuzzles the grass. The children stroke her rough brown back. "You're the best donkey in the world!" they say.

Yes, Coconut comes to school every day.

Hee-haw! Hee-haw!

she calls as she trots through the bluebell woods.

And Mr Clapper smiles at the children.

"Coconut's coming," he says.